This **ORCHARD** book belongs to

Luca
2 Hartington
RD Twickamtu'
3 en Middlesex

For Geoffrey and Jeannette and the circle they turn – S.T.

For Rachel, James, Molly and Rosa – N.S.

Author's note:
One night, many years ago,
I was at a party in a big city in Brazil
and I heard a traditional Brazilian poem
called "When a Baby is Born . . . "
This story is based on that poem.

Illustrator's note:
Classroom drawings by Emilie, Ben, Toby and Hamish
from Great Tew Primary School

ORCHARD BOOKS
338 Euston Road, London, NW1 3BH
Orchard Books Australia
Hachette Children's Books
Level 17/207 Kent Street, Sydney, NSW 2000

ISBN: 978 1 84616 511 5

First published in 2006 by Orchard Books
First published in paperback in 2007
Text © Sean Taylor 2006
Illustrations © Nick Sharratt 2006

1 3 5 7 9 10 8 6 4 2
Printed in China
Orchard Books is a division of Hachette Children's Books,
an Hachette Livre UK company.

SEAN TAYLOR   NICK SHARRATT

When a MONSTER is Born

ORCHARD BOOKS

When a **MONSTER** is born . . .

. . . there are two possibilities –

either it's a **FARAWAY-IN-THE-FORESTS** monster, or . . .

. . . it's an
UNDER-YOUR-BED monster.

If it's a **FARAWAY-IN-THE-FORESTS** monster, that's that.

But if it's an **UNDER-YOUR-BED** monster, there are two possibilities –

either it **EATS YOU**, or . . .

. . . you make friends

and **TAKE IT TO SCHOOL**.

If it **EATS YOU**, that's that.

But if you **TAKE IT TO SCHOOL**, there are two possibilities –

either it **SITS QUIETLY**, does its **HOMEWORK** and becomes the first monster to play for the **SCHOOL BASKETBALL TEAM**, or . . .

If it **SITS QUIETLY**, that's that.
But if it eats the ***HEAD TEACHER***,
there are two possibilities –

either it growls, "**YUMMY!**"
and **DANCES BOOGIE-WOOGIE**, or . . .

. . . it growls, "**SORRY!**"

and **WALKS OFF** through the wall.

If it **DANCES BOOGIE-WOOGIE**, that's that.

But if it **WALKS OFF**, there are two possibilities –

either it **SITS IN THE PARK** and scratches its head, or . . .

... it takes a deep breath and sets off

for the **FARAWAY-FORESTS**.

If it **SITS IN THE PARK**, that's that.
But if it sets off for the **FARAWAY-FORESTS,**
there are two possibilities –

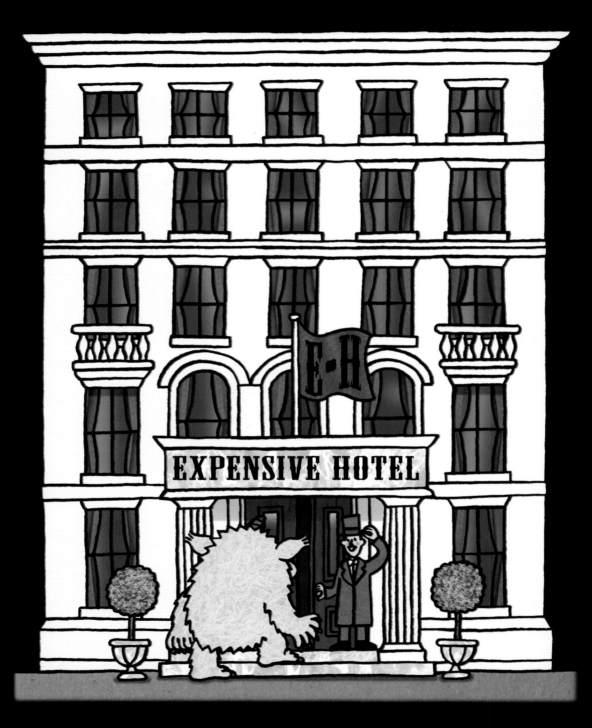

either it finds an **EXPENSIVE HOTEL**
on the way, and decides to sleep in it, or . . .

. . . it goes round the back of the hotel,
finds a **BROKEN UMBRELLA**
and decides to sleep under that.

If it sleeps in the **EXPENSIVE HOTEL**, that's that.

But if it sleeps under the **UMBRELLA**, there are two possibilities –

either a kitchen-girl comes out and tips a **SAUCEPAN OF PORRIDGE** over the monster's head, or . . .

and **STOPS IN HER TRACKS**.

STOPS IN HER TRACKS,

there are two possibilities –

either the monster gives her the
fright of her life, "**GRRROARRRR!**",
and she runs off shouting,
"**HELP! HELP! HELP!**", or . . .

. . . the monster gives her a rose

and they *FALL IN LOVE.*

If the girl runs off shouting,
"**HELP! HELP! HELP!**", that's that.

But if they *FALL IN LOVE*,
there are two possibilities –

either she kisses the monster
and it turns into a
HANDSOME YOUNG MAN, or . . .

If the monster turns into a
HANDSOME YOUNG MAN, that's that.

But if the girl turns into a
MONSTER,
there are two possibilities –

either the monster says,
"UUUUUUUUURGH!
You look horrible now!", or . . .

. . . the monster says,
"Look, I'm a monster, you're a monster.

Let's get **MARRIED**."

If the monster says,
"**UUUUUUUUURGH!**", that's that.

But if the monster says,
"Let's get **MARRIED**.",
there are two possibilities –

either the two of them live happily together
and have a **BABY MONSTER** . . .

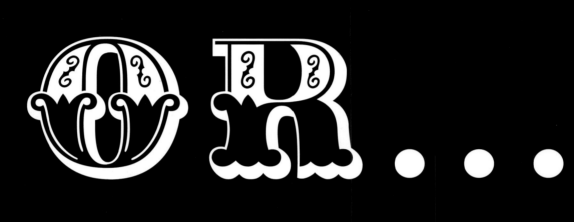

... they **EAT EACH OTHER**.

If they **EAT EACH OTHER**, that's that.

But if they have a **BABY MONSTER** there are two possibilities –

either it's a **FARAWAY-IN-THE-FOREST**

. . . it's an
UNDER-YOUR-BED monster . . .